Tales from the Arabian Nights

Enid Blyton

D1367765

Other titles by Enid Blyton
published by
Element Children's Books

Knights of the Round Table
Tales of Ancient Greece
Robin Hood Book
Bible Stories
The Land of Far-Beyond
The First Christmas
A Story Book of Jesus

Tales from the Arabian Nights

Enid Blyton

Illustrated by Jill Newton

ELEMENT
CHILDREN'S BOOKS

SHAFTESBURY, DORSET · BOSTON, MASSACHUSETTS · MELBOURNE, VICTORIA

Enid Blyton™

Text © Enid Blyton Limited 1930
All Rights Reserved

Enid Blyton's signature is a trademark of Enid Blyton Limited
For further information please contact www.blyton.com

First published in Great Britain by George Newnes in 1930
First published by Element Children's Books in 1998,
Shaftesbury, Dorset SP7 8BP
Published in the USA in 1998 by Element Books Inc.
160 North Washington Street, Boston MA 02114

Published in Australia in 1998 by Element Books Limited
and distributed by Penguin Books Australia Ltd,
487 Maroondah Highway, Ringwood, Victoria 3134

All rights reserved. No part of this publication may be reproduced or
transmitted or utilized in any form or by any means, electronic, mechanical,
photocopying or otherwise, without the prior permission of the Publisher.

The moral right of the author and illustrator have been asserted.

British Library Cataloguing in Publication data available.

Library of Congress Cataloging in Publication data available.

ISBN 1 901881 62 8

Cover design by Gabrielle Morton

Cover and inside illustrations © Jill Newton 1998

Typeset by Dorchester Typesetting Group Ltd
Printed and bound in Great Britain by Creative Print and Design

Contents

Where these stories came from

Long ago there lived a Persian sultan called Schahriah. He found that his wife had deceived him, so, in a fit of grief and anger, he killed her, vowing that he would take a new wife every evening, and cut off her head the next morning.

He kept his vow, much to the grief of the families whose daughters became his brides. Then one day the daughter of his vizier told her father that *she* wished to become the bride of the sultan.

He was horrified, and reminded her that she would be killed the day after she had married him. She said that she had a plan whereby she might be permitted to live, and at last her father agreed to tell the sultan she would wed him.

The sultan consented to marry her, but said that, even though she was the vizier's daughter, she must die in the morning. That night he married her, and she went with him willingly to his palace.

She asked that her beloved sister might sleep near her, so that she could embrace her in the morning, before she died, and the sultan gave his consent. Just before daybreak the sister, acting on the bride's plan, came to her and begged her to tell her one of her wonderful tales before the time came for her die. The sultan gave his bride permission, and she therefore began her tale.

Now she was very clever at telling stories of all kinds. She chose one that was most exciting, and the Sultan found himself listening eagerly. When the time came for her to die, the tale was not finished.

"You shall live till tomorrow morning," said the sultan. "I wish you to finish the tale tonight."

But the tale was not finished that night, nor the next, for the clever girl always ended at such an exciting part that the sultan could not bear to slay her until he knew what happened next. So she went on and on telling her tales, and every night the sultan listened with enjoyment.

For a thousand and one nights his wife told him her marvelous stories, and at the end of that time he admired her so much, and loved her so fondly, that he could not think of killing her.

"I am ashamed of my vow," he said. "You shall not die, but shall live and reign with me."

In joy and delight the sultaness threw herself at his feet and thanked him. She knew that she had not only saved herself from death, but also hundreds of maidens who might have been the one-night brides of the sultan afterwards.

In this book are some of the stories she told. They are not split up or interrupted as they were when the sultaness told them, but when you read them you can imagine the beautiful maiden reciting them to the sultan, always breaking off at the most exciting part in order to continue them the next night, and so save her life.

The Rich Merchant and the Genie

There was once a very rich merchant, who had to go on a long journey. He mounted his horse, and rode off, taking with him a small bag in which he had put some biscuits and dates.

He soon arrived at his journey's end, and completed the business that had taken him such a long way from home. Then once more he took horse and rode off, eager to return to his family.

Three days he rode in the hot sun. On the fourth day he was so tired that he turned aside to rest under some trees. He sat beneath a great walnut tree, at whose foot ran a clear stream. From his bag he took some biscuits and dates, and began to eat, throwing the date stones about him.

When he had finished his meal, he washed his face, hands, and feet, and, said his prayers, for he was a good Muhammadan. He had hardly finished doing this, and was just about to rise from his knees, when he saw an astonishing sight.

Coming towards him was a giant-like genie with a long white beard and white hair. He was of a monstrous size, and held a scimitar in his hand. At the sight of him the merchant began to tremble with fear.

"Rise up!" said the genie, in a terrible voice. "I am going to kill you as you have killed my son!"

The merchant heard these words with amazement and fear.

"How can I have killed your son?" he asked, in a voice shaking with terror. "I do not know him, and I am certain I have never seen him."

"Did you not sit down here to eat dates?" asked the genie fiercely. "Did you not throw the stones about on all sides?"

"Yes, I did," answered the merchant, in wonder.

"Then you *did* kill my son," said the monstrous genie.

"For he passed by here, and one of the stones struck him in the eye, and killed him forthwith. Therefore I shall kill you."

"Pardon me, my lord genie!" cried the merchant, in fright. "I did not see your son passing, and if I killed him, I did it unknowingly. Pardon me, I pray you, and allow me to live."

"I give no pardon," said the genie. "You shall die!"

He took the terrified merchant by the arm, and flung him down with his face to the ground, in order to cut off his head.

The man began to wail and beg for mercy so loudly that the genie did not at once let the scimitar fall, but listened.

"If you must have my life," said the poor man, "allow me to return to my wife and children and bid them good-bye. Give me a year, I beg of you, and at the end of that time I swear I will return here and you shall then do with me what you will."

"Do you take heaven to witness your promise?" asked the genie, lowering his scimitar.

"Yes," answered the man. "I do. I will swear to come back here in twelve months' time."

At this the genie suddenly disappeared, and the merchant found himself alone. Hurriedly he mounted his horse and rode home. He told his wife and children of the dreadful thing that had happened to him, and they wept bitterly when they heard of his promise to the genie.

The year flew by quickly, and soon the time came for the merchant to return to the walnut tree where he had met the genie. With great sorrow he bade goodbye to his wife and children and set off. He came at last to the tree, and sat down under it to wait for the genie, trembling with fear and misery.

As he waited, he saw an old man coming, leading a deer. He was much astonished to see him in such a lonely place, and then was even more surprised to see yet another old man who was followed by two black dogs.

They greeted one another, and the two old men asked why the merchant sat sorrowfully in such a lonely place. He told them his story, and they listened in wonder.

"I shall stay here to see what the genie does," said the first old man.

"I shall do likewise," said the other.

Then suddenly all three saw a thick mist, like a cloud of dust blown by a whirlwind, coming towards them. It disappeared, and out of its midst came the monstrous genie, his cruel scimitar in his hand. He came up to the merchant, and took him roughly by the arm.

"Get up," he said, fiercely. "I will kill you as you killed my son."

All three men began to wail and lament loudly. The

old man with the deer threw himself at the genie's feet and kissed them.

"Lord, Lord," he said, "Hearken to me. Let me tell you the story of my life, and of this deer by my side. If you think my tale is more wonderful than the adventure of this miserable merchant, I beg you to grant me one half of his body."

The genie looked at him, and stroked his long beard. Then, casting his eye on the deer, he answered, "Tell on, old man. I agree to your condition."

Without delay, the old man began his story.

The Story of the Old Man and the Deer

"This deer you see by my side," he said, "is my wife. We have been married for thirty years, and no children came to us. So at the end of twenty years I took into my family the son of a slave-woman, and brought him up as my own.

"This made my wife very jealous, although I did not know it, for she hid her hatred well. She waited patiently for a time to come when I should be away. This came when my son was ten years old, for I had to leave my family, and go on a long journey. So I went to my wife, and put the slave-woman and her son in her care, bidding her cherish them both until I came back.

"While I was gone my wife began to learn the art of magic. As soon as she knew enough for her purpose, she changed my boy into a calf, and the slave-woman into a cow. She gave the calf to my farmer, bidding him fatten it up, and also the cow.

"When I returned, I asked to see the slave and her child.

"'Your slave is dead,' said my wife. 'As for the boy, I cannot tell what has become of him. He has not been seen for two months.'

"This troubled me very much. I waited eight months for my son to return, but he did not. Then, the feast of Bairam being near, I sent to my farmer for a fat cow to sacrifice at the festival.

"He sent me one. It was no other than the unfortunate slave-woman, whom my wife had changed into a cow. As I was about to kill her, she lowed pitifully, and I was amazed to see tears streaming from her eyes.

"'I cannot kill this cow,' I said to the farmer. 'Get me another.'

"My wife, who was standing nearby, was angry when she heard this, and bade me not to be foolish.

"'Very well,' I said. 'The farmer shall kill her, for I cannot.'

"My farmer at once slew the cow, but when we skinned her, we found that, although she seemed so fat, she was nothing but bones.

"'Take her away,' I said to the farmer. 'Do with her what you will. She will not do for sacrifice. Bring me a fat calf instead.'

"The farmer went away, and soon returned, bringing with him a fine fat calf. I did not know that the

animal was my son, I could not help loving the calf when
I saw him. On his part, he grew excited as soon as he
saw me, and tried to come to me. He broke his rope, and
threw himself at my feet, doing his best to beg me to
spare him, and to show me that he was my son.

" 'I cannot sacrifice this calf,' I said. 'Take him away,
farmer, and see that you care for him properly.'

"My wife was full of anger when she heard me say
this, but I would not alter my mind. The calf listened
with tears in his eyes. Then the farmer led him away.

"Next morning the man came to me, and said he
wished to speak with me privately.

" 'Lord,' he said. 'I come to tell you a strange thing.
My daughter, who has some knowledge of magic, saw
me leading this calf away yesterday, as you bade me. She
laughed and then cried, and when I demanded to know
why, she told me truthfully.

" ' "My father," she said. "The calf you are leading is
no other than our master's son, and I laughed for joy to
see that he had not been sacrificed. I wept soon after
because I remembered how his mother, the cow, had
been killed just before." '

" 'Can this be true?' I asked the farmer, in horror and
amazement. I went at once to the shed where the calf
stood. I embraced him, and knew that he was my boy.

"Then I sent for the farmer's daughter, and asked her
if she could by magic restore my son to his proper shape.

" 'Yes, I can,' she answered, 'But only if you will grant that he may be my husband, and will allow me to punish the one who treated him so wickedly.'

"These conditions I agreed to, whereupon the girl took a vessel of water, and pronounced some strange words over it. She then threw it over the calf, who at once changed into my son.

"I ran to him, and embraced him with joy. The maiden married him, but before she did so, she punished my wife by turning her into the deer you see by my side.

"My son went traveling, and as I have not heard of him for some time, I am going in search of him. I could

not trust my wife to anyone while I was gone, so I have brought her with me, as you see. Now do you not think, O genie, that my story is even more wonderful than that of this miserable merchant at my side?"

"It is truly as you say," said the genie, who had listened marveling to the tale. "I grant you half the man's body."

"Listen now to *my* tale," said the old man with the two black dogs. "If you think it more wonderful than the tale of the deer, pray grant me the other half of this merchant's body."

"Tell on," said the genie. So the old man began.

The Story of the Old Man and the Two Black Dogs

"Great prince," he said, "these two black dogs you see are my brothers. When our father died he left us a thousand sequins each, and we all became merchants.

"My eldest brother soon sold his estate, and went traveling, intending to trade in far-off countries. At the end of a year a poor man came to my shop.

"I thought he had come to beg for money, and I greeted him.

"'God keep you,' I said.

"'And you also,' he said. 'Is it possible, brother, that you do not know me?'

"Then I saw, to my grief, that the poor man was none other than my unfortunate brother, who had lost all his money in his travels, and was now come back to beg help from me. As I had doubled my thousand sequins, I made haste to give him half.

"Soon after this my second brother sold his estate, and joined a caravan to go trading. But alas! At the end of a year he also returned, all his money gone. I had again made my thousand sequins into two, and willingly I gave him a thousand for himself, to make up his loss.

"Some time later my two brothers came to me, and besought me to go trading with them in a ship. For a long time I refused, but they pressed me so hard that at last I gave way. But when we came to buy the goods to take with us in the ship, I found that they had spent all the thousand sequins I had given to each of them, and had none left. So it fell to me to take my own money and spend that.

"I had six thousand sequins by now. I spent three thousand of them in goods, and hid the other three in a corner of my house.

"'For,' I said to my brothers, 'when you have gone trading before, you have lost all. If the same misfortune befalls us this time, we shall at least have a thousand sequins each, waiting for us at home.'

"Then we set off in our ship. After a month's sail we came to a port, where we landed. We sold our goods to much profit, mine especially.

"Just as we were about to embark again, I met a

maiden on the seashore. She was very beautiful, but her
dress was old and ragged. She greeted me, and much to
my surprise begged me to marry her. I would not consent, but she kissed my hand, and prayed me so hard to
take her with me, that at last I said I would.

"I bought her some fine dresses, and married her
before embarking on my ship. As the days went on I
found that she was as good as she was beautiful, and I
loved her more and more.

"My two brothers began to be very jealous of me.
They were angry because I had sold my goods at a better
price than theirs; they could not bear to see me so happy
with my beautiful wife. So one night, when we were
both asleep, they took us and threw us into the sea.

"Now, I should surely have been drowned if it had not
been for my wife. I had hardly touched the water when

she took me up, and bore me to an island. I was amazed, but when I heard what she had to say, I was even more surprised.

"'I am a fairy,' she said. 'When I saw you about to embark on your ship, I fell in love with you. I disguised myself as a poor woman, to see if you would have pity on me. You were kind and generous, and I am glad to repay you for your good nature. But as for those two brothers of yours, I shall slay them!'

"I thanked the fairy for her goodness to me, but begged her not to have vengeance on my brothers.

"'Pardon them,' I said. 'I do not wish their death, even though they have tried to drown me.'

"Then I told her all I had done for them – but when she heard, she flew into such a terrible rage that nothing would pacify her but to fly after them, and sink their ship.

"'No, fair lady,' I said. 'Remember they are my brothers. We must return good for evil, so calm your anger.'

"Very soon the fairy transported me from the island to the roof of my house, and then disappeared. I went to the corner where my three thousand sequins were hidden, and took them. Then I made my way to my shop, which I opened, and began to trade as my custom was.

"When I returned to my house, I was surprised to see two black dogs there. They came up to me, and lay down at my feet. They tried in every way to show me that I

was their master, and I
could not think where
they had come from.

"Then suddenly the
fairy appeared again.

"'Husband,' she said,
'do not be surprised at
these two black dogs.
They are your brothers.'

"'My brothers!' I
exclaimed. 'How came
they to be changed into dogs?'

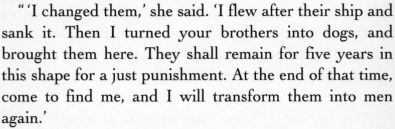

"'I changed them,' she said. 'I flew after their ship and
sank it. Then I turned your brothers into dogs, and
brought them here. They shall remain for five years in
this shape for a just punishment. At the end of that time,
come to find me, and I will transform them into men
again.'

"With that she vanished from my sight.

"The five years are now ended, so I am traveling in
search of my fairy wife, taking with me my two brothers
who, as you see, are still black dogs. Now, O lord genie,
do you not think my story is even more marvelous than
that of the old man with the deer?"

"Yes," said the genie. "I own it. Take your half of the
merchant's body, and do what you will with it."

So saying, he disappeared utterly, to the great delight

of all three men.

"Keep my half of your body for yourself!" said the old man with the deer.

"And mine also," said the old man with the two black dogs. "Thus you are saved from death, O merchant."

The grateful man thanked his two friends with tears in his eyes. Then he said goodbye to them, and each went on his way. The merchant returned home to his wife and children, and lived happily ever after.

The Fisherman and the King of the Black Isles

O nce upon a time there was an old fisherman, so poor that he had scarcely enough money to keep his wife and three children. Every day he went to fish in the sea. He cast his nets four times only, for it was his rule to do no more than that each day.

One morning, very early, when the moon still rode in the sky, he took his nets and went down to the sea. He cast them into the water, and then threw them towards the shore. He felt them to be very heavy, and he rejoiced, thinking he had a fine catch of fish.

But he soon found that he had caught nothing but the carcass of an ass. A second time he cast his nets, and again found them heavy. He drew them in, and discovered he had got a wicker basket full of stones and mud. In great disappointment he mended his torn net, and threw it into the water a third time.

Once more his net became heavy, but alas for the poor man! Stones, slime, and sand filled the meshes, and he was nearly mad with despair, for now he had but one more time to throw his net.

A fourth time he cast it, waited a little, and drew it in. It felt very heavy, and was difficult to drag to shore. The fisherman rejoiced, for he thought surely he had been lucky at last. He looked eagerly in the net, but saw no fish. Instead he found a big jar made of yellow copper, which seemed by its weight to be full of something.

The jar was tightly fastened and sealed with lead. The fisherman took it out of the net, and looked at it with joy.

"I can sell this jar!" he said. "With the money I get I shall buy a measure of corn."

He looked at the seal on it, and wondered if anything precious was inside. He shook it, but could hear nothing rattle. He took out his knife, and broke the seal. Then he turned the jar upside down to see what would come out of it.

But to his surprise nothing came out at all. This puzzled the old man, for he could not think why it felt so heavy, or was so well sealed, if there was nothing inside. He turned it the right way up, and stood it on a rock, looking at it closely.

Suddenly a very thick smoke began to stream out of the mouth of the jar. The fisherman stepped back in astonishment, and watched it. It rose as high as the clouds, and spread all over the sea and the shore, making a great mist. The old man gaped at it, startled and amazed.

When all the smoke was out of the jar, it began to collect itself together, until it became a solid body. Then the fisherman saw that it had taken the shape of a genie,

twice as big as the
greatest of giants. He
was so terrified that
he tried to run away,
but his legs would not
carry him.

Then the genie spoke.
"Solomon, Solomon!"
he cried. "Pardon me,
I beseech you! I will
henceforth obey you!"

The fisherman heard
him in amazement.

"What is this you say?" he said. "Do you
not know that Solomon has been dead for hundreds of
years?"

"Speak to me more civilly!" answered the genie
fiercely. "Or I will kill you."

"But what have I done that you should kill me?"
asked the poor fisherman. "Have I not done you the
great service of freeing you from your imprisonment in
that jar?"

"I shall kill you because of a vow I have made,"
answered the genie. "Listen to my story. King Solomon
shut me up in the jar, because I would not obey him. He
threw it into the deep sea, and there I remained for centuries. Now the first hundred years I was in the jar I

vowed that whoever should free me should be rewarded by wealth. The second hundred years I vowed that my rescuer should have all the treasure of the earth. The third hundred years I promised that whoever freed me should become a powerful monarch, and that I would be his servant, and grant him three wishes every day, no matter what they might be.

"But the centuries went by, and still I was a prisoner. Then I became angry, and vowed that whoever should free me should die immediately. You must therefore be killed."

The fisherman listened and trembled with fear. He begged for mercy, but the genie scorned his pleading. Then a cunning plan came into the poor man's mind.

"Before I die," he said, "I beg you to tell me one thing – were you really in that small jar?"

'You know that I was," answered the genie.

"I can hardly believe you," said the fisherman. "Why, not even one of your feet would go into the jar, so how could your whole body be there?"

"I swear to you that I was in the jar," said the genie angrily. "How can you say that you do not believe me?"

"I certainly shall doubt your word unless you show me that you truly *were* in the jar," said the fisherman. "It is impossible!"

At that the angry genie began to dissolve himself into smoke again, and soon streamed into the jar, until not even a wisp was left. Then a voice came out of the neck, saying: "Well, now unbelieving man, I am all in the jar. Do you still doubt what I say?"

The fisherman made no answer, but swiftly took the lid of the jar, and screwed it on tightly.

"Ha!" he cried in joy. "Now it is *your* turn to beg for mercy, genie! I shall throw the jar back into the deep sea again, and warn all poor fishermen against freeing you, should they catch the jar in their nets!"

The genie saw that he had been tricked, and besought the fisherman to free him again. He tried to get out of the jar, but he could not.

"Fisherman," he said, in kindly tones, "free me once more, and I will make you a rich man."

The fisherman longed to be wealthy, and he listened to the genie's promises. But he did not trust the monster, and refused to free him unless the genie swore to him in the great name of God that he would keep his word.

This the genie did, and since the fisherman felt certain that he would not dare to break such an oath as that, he took off the lid of the jar once more. Out came the smoke again, and soon the genie was there before the old man, who trembled a second time to see his huge form towering above him.

The first thing the genie did was to kick the jar right into the sea. He saw the look of fear that came into the fisherman's face, and laughed.

"Do not be afraid," he said. "I will keep my word to you. You shall be rich. Take up your nets, and follow me."

The old man did as he was bid. The genie led him past the town up to the top of a mountain. Then they climbed down to the plain, and after a time came to a great pond that lay between four hills.

"Cast your nets in this water," commanded the genie.

The fisherman did so, and caught four fish. They were curious creatures, for one was white, one yellow, one blue, and one red.

"Take these fish to the sultan," said the genie. "He will give you gold for them. You may come here each day and cast your nets once, but no more."

With that he smote the ground with his foot. The earth opened, and the genie vanished utterly.

The fisherman, amazed at all his adventures, took up the four fishes, and made his way to the sultan's palace. He presented them to the sultan, who was delighted with them. He looked at them in wonder, and commanded that they should be cooked for his dinner.

Then he gave the fisherman four hundred pieces of gold, and bade him go. The old man, amazed at so much wealth, made his way home in a dream, planning what he should buy for his family.

The sultan's cook-maid took the fish, and began to fry them. She put them into a frying-pan with oil, and when they were done on one side, she turned them over. But she had no sooner done this than the wall of the kitchen suddenly opened, and out came a maiden of marvelous beauty, clad in shining satin, and arrayed with jewels.

She carried a stick of myrtle in her hand, and with this she struck the four fish.

"Fish, fish," she said, "do you do your duty?"

At first the fish answered nothing, so she struck them again, and questioned them. Then they lifted up their heads, and answered her.

"Yes, yes," they said. "If you reckon, we reckon. If you pay your debts, we pay ours. If you fly, we conquer, and are happy."

When she heard this, the maiden overturned the frying-pan, and entered the opening in the wall, which shut, and became just as it was before.

The cook-maid was very much frightened. She picked up the four fish, but saw that they were not fit to take to the sultan. She began to weep and wail with fright.

Soon the vizier came to see why the fish were so long in cooking, and the weeping cook-maid told him what had happened. He listened in amazement, and ran to tell the sultan.

"Send for the fisherman and bid him bring me four more such fish," commanded the sultan. This was done, and the fisherman promised to bring them as soon as he could. He went to the pond, cast in his nets, and brought out four fish as before. He took them to the sultan, who gave him another four hundred pieces of gold.

Then the sultan shut himself up in his room with the vizier, and began to fry the fish. No sooner had he turned them on their sides than the wall opened, and out came a monstrous black slave with a green wand in his hand. He went to the fish and struck them, asking them, in a terrible voice, if they were doing their duty.

They answered as before. The slave upset the pan on the floor, entered the hole in the wall, and disappeared.

"This is a most amazing thing." said the sultan, greatly astonished. "I am determined to know all that lies behind these strange fish. Send for the fisherman again."

Once more the old man came to the palace. The sultan commanded him to show the way to the pond from which he took the fish, and the fisherman obeyed.

All the sultan's court went with him, and were much amazed when they saw the pond lying between the four hills.

"This is strange," said the vizier. "For sixty years I have hunted in the land round about, but never before have I seen this pond, nor these hills."

The Sultan saw that the pond was full of the many-
coloured fish, and he wondered how the water came to
be there with all the strange fish in it. He called his
vizier to him, and spoke to him.

"I have a mind to solve this mystery," he said. "I may
be away some days, so do not be alarmed."

He put on a strong suit, took his scimitar in his hand,

and when night came, left the pond and walked towards one of the four hills. He climbed it, and found a plain beyond. When the sun rose he was down on the plain, and saw some distance away a great building.

He found that it was a strong castle of black marble, highly polished, and covered with fine steel as bright as a mirror. He went to the gates, and knocked loudly many times; but no one came.

"This is strange," said the sultan. "Well, I will enter. If no one is within, I have nothing to fear. If someone is there, I have my scimitar with which to defend myself."

He entered the gates, and, coming to the door of the castle, cried out in a loud voice, saying that a stranger begged for food. No one came forward to receive him, so he went through the door into the castle.

There were great halls there, furnished richly with tapestries and silken hangings, and embroidered in silver and gold. Every apartment was grand and magnificent. The outer ones looked out on marvelous gardens where were fountains, flowers, and trees, among which flew wonderful singing birds.

The sultan sat down on a veranda, and looked out with pleasure on this beautiful garden. Suddenly he heard a sound of weeping and wailing, and grief-stricken cries came to his ears. He listened in wonder.

"Oh Fortune!" wailed the voice, "I am the most unhappy man in the world. Let me no longer live, but grant me a speedy death!"

The sultan leapt to his feet, and went to the door hung with a silken curtain. He drew it aside, and saw a large room, at the end of which sat a richly-dressed young man on a throne. It was he who was lamenting so bitterly.

The sultan approached him and bowed. The young man looked at him sorrowfully.

"My lord," he said, "I wish I could return your greeting, and rise to welcome you. But alas! I cannot!"

"That is nothing," said the sultan. "Now tell me, I pray you, the reason for your cries. Can I not help you? And what is the meaning of the pond where the many-coloured fishes are, and of this lonely castle, and, last of all, why are you here all alone?"

The young man did not answer these questions. Instead he began to weep bitterly, and raised up his robe. Then the amazed sultan saw that the prince was a man only to his waist, for from there to his feet he was changed into black marble.

He started back in horror, and bade the young man tell him all his tale.

"Listen then," said the young king mournfully, "and I will tell you a strange story."

The History of the Young King of the Black Isles

"This is the kingdom of the Black Isles, which takes its

name from those four little hills, which were once islands. Its capital stood where you now see the great pond.

"My father ruled over this kingdom till his death. I then came to the throne, and married a beautiful maiden, my cousin. For five years we lived happily, and then I found that she no longer loved me.

"One day I felt sleepy after dinner, and laid myself down to rest. Two of my wife's ladies came and sat down by me, one at my head, and one at my feet, to keep the flies away with their fans. They thought I was fast asleep, and began to talk to one another in whispers.

"'How can the queen not love such a kind husband as this?' said one.

"'It is very strange,' replied the other. 'I know that she goes out every night, and leaves him alone. How is it that he does not notice this?'

"'She makes sure that he does not!' said the first lady. 'She puts a certain herb in his evening drink, which causes him to sleep soundly all night through. Therefore he does not know when she leaves him or where she goes. When day dawns she returns, and by placing some scent beneath his nose, she awakes him.'

"I listened in astonishment and dismay. I pretended to awake from sleep, and the ladies ceased their talk. Then my wife came in, and we supped together.

"She mixed me my evening drink, but this time I did

not drink it. Instead I went to an open window, and emptied the cup outside. Then I put it into her hands, and she thought I had drunk the potion.

"That night, when she judged me to be sound asleep, she arose and dressed herself.

"'Sleep, and may you never wake again!' she hissed, for she had no idea that I was awake. Then she went swiftly from the room.

"At once I arose, took my scimitar, and followed her quickly. She went through several gates, each of which opened before her silently when she spoke some magic words. Last of all she passed through the garden gate, and then entered a little wood guarded by a thick hedge. I followed, and hid myself.

"I saw that she had met a man, and was speaking words of love to him. She offered to turn the city and palace into ruins, to show him how strong was her love for him. At this I was enraged, and, darting from my hiding place, I struck at him with my scimitar, fatally wounding him.

"Then, before the queen knew who I was, I swiftly returned to the palace, and laid myself down in bed again. She ran to the help of her lover, and by her enchantments succeeded in keeping death away. But although he was alive, he could not move nor speak, so that he seemed more dead than living.

"I fell asleep, and when I awoke the queen was at my

side. She had dressed herself in mourning, and her hair was hanging about her eyes.

"'Sir, do not be surprised at my sad appearance,' she said. 'I have had sorrowful news today. The queen, my mother, is dead. My father the king has been killed in battle, and my brother has fallen into a river, and is drowned.'

"I pretended to believe her story, though I very well knew why she was so distressed. She mourned for a whole year, and then came to me with a request.

"'Allow me to build myself a tomb in the palace grounds, she begged. 'There I will remain to the end of my days.'

"I gave my consent, and she built herself a stately palace, and called it the Palace of Tears. She commanded that her half-dead lover should be taken there, and this was done. Every day she took him the magic potion which kept him alive, but no matter what she did she could not make him any better.

"He could not walk, speak, or move, but could only look at her. The queen made him two long visits every day, and though I pretended to know nothing of this, I was aware of everything that passed.

"One day I went to the Palace of Tears myself. I hid behind a curtain, and heard the queen speak loving words to her gallant, beseeching him to answer her. She wept and groaned until I lost all patience, and rushed

out from behind the curtain.

"'Wicked woman,' I said, 'cease your sighing and groaning. I should have killed you when I struck down this wretch.'

"I raised my scimitar, but she regarded me with a jeering smile.

"'Stay your anger,' she said. Then she immediately chanted some magic words which I did not understand.

"'And now, by virtue of my enchantments,' she added, 'I command you to become half marble and half man!'

"At once I became what you now see me – half man, half marble, neither living nor yet dead.

"The enchantress brought me to this hall and placed me here. Then by her fearful magic she destroyed my capital city, with all its houses, shops, and fine buildings, and turned it into the pond you saw. The people she changed into fishes. The white are the Muhammadans; the red are the Persians, who are worshipers of fire; the blue are Christians; and the yellow are Jews. To add to my sorrow, this wicked woman comes every day and lashes my naked back a hundred times with a whip."

The young king began to weep bitterly as he came to the end of his strange story, and the sultan was so grieved that he could not say one word to comfort him.

"I will revenge you," he said at last. "Be of good cheer, for I will think of a plan whereby you shall be delivered from your unhappiness."

Then, as night was come, the sultan lay down to rest, but the poor young king did not sleep, for he had been unable to do so ever since his enchantment.

Before dawn came the sultan arose, and made his way to the Palace of Tears. He found it lit with many torches, and scented with delicious perfumes. On the bed lay the half-dead magician of whom the queen was so fond. The sultan put the poor wretch out of his misery and threw his body down a well in the courtyard.

Then he went and lay down in the bed, putting his

scimitar under the counterpane, and waited for the queen to come.

After the enchantress had given her miserable husband a hundred lashes with her whip, she entered the Palace of Tears, and leaned over the bed.

"Alas, my love!" she groaned. "Will you never speak to me again? How I long to hear your voice once more!"

The sultan pretended to awaken from a long sleep, and spoke a few words in a low and feeble voice. The queen heard him, and cried out in rapture:

"My dear lord, do I really hear your voice? Speak to me again, I pray you!"

"Wretched woman," answered the sultan, "you are not worthy to be spoken to!"

The queen began to weep.

"Why do you speak to me so reproachfully?" she asked. "What have I done to make you angry?"

"Do you not know that the cries and wails of your husband have hindered me from being cured?" said the wily sultan. "Unless you restore the king to well-being, I shall never be able to speak to you again."

The queen immediately ran out of the Palace of Tears. She took a cup of water, and said some magic words over it, whereupon it began to boil furiously. She then went to her poor husband, and threw it over him.

"Change back to your natural form!" she commanded. At once the young king felt the enchantment leave him, and he saw that he was now a man from his head to his heels, and no longer half marble. He arose up in the greatest joy.

"Go!" said the queen fiercely, "and never return to this castle again, or I will slay you!"

The young man at once went to a place some distance away, and there awaited the coming of the sultan. Meanwhile, the queen returned to the Palace of Tears, and spoke fondly to the sultan, thinking that he was her lover.

"Dear lord," she said, "I have done your bidding."

"You have not done enough," said the sultan. "Do you not know that at midnight all the fishes in the pond raise their heads, and cry out for vengeance against me and you? Transform the pond back into the city it once was, and change the fishes into people. Then and then only can I be cured. When you have done this, come to me, and you shall give me your hand and help me to arise."

Full of joy to hear this, the queen hastened to do what she was commanded. She ran to the pond, and taking a little water in her hand, sprinkled it around, at the same time pronouncing magic words over the fishes and the pond.

In a trice a wonderful change took place. The pond became the great city it once was, and all the fishes were restored to their proper shape, and became people. In fact, everything became as it had been before the enchantment.

The sultan's court, which had been encamped on the edge of the pond, were amazed to find the water disappear, and a great city spring up around them. They gazed about in wonder, and marveled loudly.

The enchantress returned swiftly to the Palace of Tears. "My lord!" she cried, "your commands are all fulfilled. Give me your hand."

"Come near me," said the sultan.

She approached him. He arose suddenly from the bed, and with one blow of his scimitar struck the wicked queen dead. Then he hastened to find the young king.

"Young man!" he said, "rejoice and fear no more. Your enemy is dead!"

The young man could not find enough words with which to thank the brave sultan.

"Say no more," begged the sultan. "You may now rule happily in your own land, or, if you wish, you may accompany me to mine, which is not far away, and where you will be much welcomed."

"Great lord," said the young king, "you are mistaken in thinking that your land is but a few hours away. It may have been, when my own kingdom was enchanted, but now that it is restored to its own place and form, it is at least a year's journey away!"

This the astonished sultan found to be true. He was sad to think that he would be so far from the young man when he returned to his own land, and he begged him to accompany him, and to be his son.

"For," said he, "I have no child of my own, and if you will come with me, you shall be king after me."

This the young man agreed to, for he felt the greatest love for his deliverer. His cousin was made king of the Black Isles in his stead, and he himself went with the sultan on the long year's journey.

When they arrived, the people of the sultan's kingdom gave them a great welcome, and for many days there was feasting and merry-making. The sultan took the young king for his son, and each of them was happy in the other.

As for the old fisherman, whose finding of the copper jar had caused such strange adventures, he was greatly rewarded. The sultan gave him a fine estate, and there he and his family lived happily to the end of their lives.

The Story of Sindbad the Sailor

The Strange Little Island

Let me tell you my story. I am Sindbad, a sailor whose adventures will fill you with amazement, for each of the six voyages I have taken have been full of marvels of many kinds.

My father died when I was young, and left me much wealth. Most of this I spent foolishly. Then, when I was almost in poverty, I took the advice of some friends and went to sea. I took with me some goods which I hoped to sell at a profit when we touched at a port.

I embarked at Balsora, a port on the Persian Gulf. We set sail, and in due course arrived at several islands, where we sold or exchanged our goods. Then one day the wind dropped, and we lay becalmed near a little island which was almost level with the surface of the water. It looked like a smooth, green meadow, and some of us resolved to land upon it, and stretch our legs.

We had not been on the curious little island very long before it suddenly began to quake and tremble. Those on board the ship saw this, and shouted to us to beware – for we were on no island, but on the back of a huge whale!

Some jumped into the boat near by, and others swam to the ship. When the whale suddenly dived, I was the only person left on its back.

I had time to catch hold of a piece of driftwood, and then had to struggle for my life. The captain took up those who were in the boat, and rescued those who were swimming, but did not see me. A favorable wind sprang up at that moment, and I saw, to my great horror, all the sails of my ship hoisted. Then the ship drove off before the wind, and I was left in the sea alone.

I struggled in the water for a day and a night, and should certainly have been drowned if a big wave had not taken me and thrown me on an island. I lay on the shore half dead, and waited for the sun to rise and warm me.

When I had a little recovered, I went to seek food and water. I found some herbs to eat, and a spring of clear, cool water. Then, to my surprise, I came across a beautiful horse tied to a post.

It was a fine mare, and as I approached I was astonished to hear a voice calling me from under the ground. I turned and saw a man coming from a cave. He asked who I was, and how I came there, and I told him of my adventure.

He took me into the cave, where I found more men. I asked them who they were, and they told me.

"We are the grooms of King Mihrage," they said. "Every year we bring his mares to this part of the island. Tomorrow we return, so if we had not found you today, you would surely have perished, for no one lives in this spot."

The next day they took me with them to the city where King Mihrage dwelt. They presented me to him, and he asked me all my story, which I told him truthfully.

"You shall stay here in safety," he said. "I will command that you want for nothing."

He was as good as his word. I was well looked after, and had everything I needed.

When merchants came to the town I went to talk with them, hoping to hear news of my own city of Bagdad, or to find some way of going back there; for the city of King Mihrage is on the sea, and has a fine port, to which come vessels from all parts of the world.

One day, when I was at the port, a ship arrived. The merchants on board commanded that the bales of goods should be carried ashore. I watched them, and looked for the name on each. Judge of my astonishment when I saw my own name, Sindbad, on some of them, and knew them to be the very goods I had embarked at Balsora!

I looked at the captain, and knew him. But as I felt certain he thought I was drowned, I asked him whose bales these were.

"They belonged to a merchant called Sindbad, who was unhappily drowned," he replied. "I am now going to sell them, and give the money to his family."

"Captain," said I, "those bales belong to me, for I am that Sindbad whom you thought to be drowned."

"What impudence is this!" cried the captain. "With my own eyes I saw Sindbad drawn under the waves."

"Patience, patience," I said. "Hear my tale, and then judge whether or no I am Sindbad."

Whereupon I told him all my adventures. He listened in amazement, and called some of the passengers of his ship. They knew me, and embraced me with joy and wonder.

Then the captain himself remembered me, and embraced me gladly.

"Heaven be praised for your lucky escape!" he said. "Here are all your goods. Take and do with them what you wish."

I went to King Mihrage, and told him of my good fortune. I gave him a valuable present from my goods, bade him farewell, and embarked once more on my ship. We set sail, and went off before the wind.

By the time I once more reached the port of Balsora, I had sold my goods to such profit that I had a hundred thousand sequins to my name. My family were overjoyed to see me, and embraced me tenderly.

Then I bought many slaves, and built myself a great house. Here I settled down, eager to enjoy the pleasures of life, and to forget what I had suffered.

The Giant Roc and the Valley of Diamonds

For some time I had a quiet and peaceful life. But soon I tired of this, and longed to go to sea again. I bought some goods, embarked on another ship, and began my second voyage.

We touched island after island, and sold our goods to great profit. Then one day we came to an isle where grew many fine fruit trees, but as far as we could see, there were no people there at all.

We landed, and began to roam about. I sat down by a stream, and soon fell fast asleep.

When I awoke, the ship was gone! I got up and looked about for the men who had been with me on the island, but could see them nowhere. Then, far on the skyline, I saw the ship, and soon she had disappeared altogether.

I thought I should die of dismay and sorrow. I beat

my head and breast, and cried out in despair. Then I
bethought myself to climb a tree, and see from there if I
was near any town.

On the sea side was nothing but sea and sky, but on
the land side I saw something white, though I could not
tell what it was. I climbed down, and made my way
towards this.

When I came near I thought it must be a great bowl of
some sort, very high and very big. I touched it, and

found it smooth. I walked round it, but there was no opening anywhere. It was at least fifty paces round. I could not think what it might be.

Then suddenly the sky seemed to grow dark. I looked up and saw a monstrous bird flying towards me. It flew down to the ground, and sat upon the great white thing – which I at once knew to be its egg!

I knew then that the bird must be a gigantic roc, of which I had heard mariners tell many tales. A plan came to me, and I swiftly unwrapped the folds of my turban. With it I tied myself tightly to the great bird's legs, which seemed to me like the trunks of trees, and waited for it to fly away. I thought that then I should be taken from this barren place.

Next morning the bird flew off, taking me with her. She flew very high, and I could not see the earth. Then she began to fly downwards at such a terrible pace that I fainted. When I opened my eyes again, I found myself on the ground with the great roc. I at once untied myself, and no sooner had I done so than the bird rose into the air again, having in her beak an enormous serpent.

I looked round and saw that I was in a deep valley. It was surrounded by such high, steep mountains that I saw at once I could not climb them. How then was I to get out? I seemed to be even worse off than when I was on the desert island.

As I walked about I saw that diamonds were strewn over the ground. Some of these were so enormous that I looked on them with delight. But I soon saw something that took all my pleasure away – for in the distance were serpents, huger than any I had ever seen or heard of. Even the smallest of them could have swallowed an elephant!

I walked about all day, and when night drew near I found a small cave where I thought I should be safe from

the snakes. I went inside, and shut up the mouth of it with a large stone. It did not quite close the cave, but allowed a little daylight to enter. When it was quite dark I lay down to sleep.

But the serpents came all round my cave, and I could hear them hissing in a fearful manner. I was so afraid that I could not even close my eyes. I was glad when daylight entered the cave, and the snakes glided away. They feared the giant rocs, and went to hide themselves.

Trembling, I pushed the stone away, and went out into the valley once more. I had passed such a terrible night that I walked on the diamonds without giving them a thought. Then, as I was very tired and sleepy, I sat down, and thought I would sleep for a while.

I had no sooner shut my eyes than I was awakened by something rolling by me with a great noise. I jumped to my feet, and saw to my surprise that a large piece of fresh meat had rolled by me. As I looked at it in amazement, I saw several other pieces coming down from the rocks in the mountains.

Then I knew that I was in the famous Valley of Diamonds which had never been trodden by the foot of man, owing to the steep mountains that protect it. I knew also the meaning of the pieces of meat, for I had many times heard of the trick that merchants used in order to get diamonds from this valley.

There are many eagles in this country, and in the sea-son when they nest and have young ones, the merchants throw large joints of meat into the valley of Diamonds. These roll over many precious stones, which stick to them. The eagles pounce on the meat and carry it away in their claws to their nests. The merchants run to the nests, frighten away the eagles, and then take the diamonds out of the meat. Thus do they enrich themselves.

Up till that moment I had thought that never should I be able to get out of the valley; but when I saw the meat rolling by me, an idea came into my mind, and I rejoiced. I swiftly gathered up the biggest diamonds I could see, and filled my wallet with them. Then I went to the largest piece of meat in the valley, and tied myself to it with the long rolls of my turban.

I lay face downwards, waiting for the coming of the eagles. Soon I felt one pick me up in its strong claw, and bear me away to the mountain-top. As soon as it had placed me in its nest, the merchants began shouting to frighten it away. Then they ran to see if there were any diamonds in the meat.

When they saw me, they were very much alarmed, but soon they began abusing me, saying that I had stolen their diamonds.

"Speak civilly to me," I bade them. "I have here far more diamonds than any of you. *You* have to take what the eagles bring you – but I have chosen my diamonds myself, from the bottom of the valley."

I showed them my wallet, and told them how I had escaped from the valley, whereat they all marveled. They took me to the place where they were staying together, and there I begged the merchant in whose nest I had been found (for each merchant had his own) to take as many of my big diamonds as he pleased. But he would take only one, and that the smallest of all.

"For," he said, "this one alone will make me rich enough to settle down in peace and happiness for the rest of my days."

After a while we all started off to return to our own land. We had many adventures on the way, but arrived at last at Balsora, from where I went to Bagdad. From my great wealth I gave much money to the poor, and then once again settled down to enjoy peace and comfort after my strange adventures.

The Black Giant and the Great Serpent

I soon grew tired of my peaceful life, and longed to go voyaging again. So one day I bought some choice goods, and embarked for the third time at Balsora. When our journey was about half over, we ran into a fearful tempest which went on for several days, and drove us off course.

We came to an island, which the captain seemed very loath to approach, but there was no help for it. We entered the port, cast anchor, and furled our sails.

"This island and those round about are infested by a fearful multitude of men," said the captain. "They will attack us, and we must be careful not to defend ourselves nor to kill any of them, or they will swarm over us and destroy us all."

No sooner had he spoken than we saw the men swimming towards us. They were tiny savages, about two feet high, very ugly, and covered with thick red hair. There were so many of them that none of us could count them. They climbed up our ship, took down the sails, and cut away the anchor.

We watched them, and trembled, for we did not dare to defend ourselves. They hauled our ship to shore, and after making us get out, they took it away.

We made our way into the island, and found some herbs and fruit. Then, away in the distance we saw a great palace, with a double gate of ebony. We went through this, and found ourselves in a courtyard. On one side was a heap of human bones, and on the other a great number of roasting-spits.

We were struck with horror at this sight, and fell flat to the ground, unable to move for fear.

Then, just as we were in this plight, the gate opened, and in came a great black giant, as high as a palm tree. He had one burning red eye in the middle of his fore-head, and his fore-teeth stuck right out of his mouth. His under-lip hung down on his chest, and his great ears flapped over his shoulders.

We were so frightened at the sight of this monster that we lay as if we were dead.

When we came to ourselves, we saw the giant sitting nearby, watching us. Then he suddenly caught me up in his hand, and turned me round and round. But as I was very lean, he put me down again. He looked at all the others, and seeing that the captain was the fattest, he ate him for his supper.

This terrified us exceedingly. We heard the monster snoring all night long, but when morning came, he arose and departed. We were so frightened that we could think of no way to save ourselves. We ran about the island, taking herbs and fruit where we found them, but at night we returned to the palace, for there was no place to lie in but that.

The giant came in again, and ate another of our companions. We could do nothing but lament bitterly. The next day we determined to think of a plan of escape. I had noticed much driftwood about, and this gave me an idea.

"Let us make ourselves small rafts," I said. "Then we can perhaps throw ourselves on the mercy of the sea if no ship comes by to rescue us."

The others thought this a good idea, and we spent the day in making rafts, each big enough to take three people. At night we returned to the palace, where once more the giant ate yet another of our company.

This enraged us so much that we determined to be revenged upon the monster. So when he was asleep we heated the ends of nine roasting-spits in the fire till they were red-hot. Then we thrust them into the giant's eye and blinded him.

He awoke in great pain, and began to cry out, and to grope round for us, but we hid ourselves well, and he could not find us. At last he flung open the ebony gate and ran out howling. We followed, and made our way to the shore, resolving to wait until day, and then put out to sea on our little rafts.

Just as day dawned we saw the blind giant appear, with two others leading him. Behind came a great number of other monsters. As soon as we saw them we jumped on our rafts, and pushed off from shore. The giants saw us, and picked up great stones. These they threw at us, and their aim was so good that they sank all the rafts except the one upon which I and my two companions were.

We rowed as fast as we could, and at last we were out of reach of the giants. But then, alas! we were at the mercy of the wind and waves. We were tossed about for two days and nights, and then saw to our joy that we were

being driven upon an island.

We landed in safety, and found some fruit to eat, and water to drink. Then we went to sleep on the sea-shore. We were awakened by a rustling noise, and to our horror saw an immense serpent. It swallowed up one of my companions, and in the greatest terror we fled away.

We came to a tall tree, and climbed it to be out of reach of the serpent, should it come that way. It was not long before the snake came hissing to the foot of the tree, and seeing us there, raised itself up against the trunk, and swallowed my comrade, who was a little lower than I was.

I was terrified, and remained in the tree for a long while. When at last I climbed down I fully expected to meet the same fate as my friends. The snake was not to be seen, however, so I hurriedly began to make myself some protection from it.

I gathered together small branches, thorns, and brambles, and bound them into faggots. These I placed all round me in a circle, and also tied some above my head in the tree. Then when night came I shut myself up in the circle. Soon the snake came along, hissing fiercely. It glided round and round the thorny rampart, but could not get in.

After a time it rolled up, and lay still, waiting for me to come forth. But this I did not do, and when day dawned the serpent glided away, and left me in safety.

I was so tired, and had suffered so much from the creature's poisonous breath, that I was full of despair. I ran down to the sea, meaning to throw myself into the water, when suddenly, to my great joy, I saw a ship passing in the distance!

I shouted, and waved my turban. The crew saw me, and the captain sent out a boat to take me. Everyone crowded round me when I arrived on the ship's deck,

and asked me how I came to be on the island. I soon
related my adventures, and the crew rejoiced that they
had rescued me. The captain gave me one of his own
suits, for I was all in rags.

Then the ship sailed onwards again. We touched at
many ports, and at last came to Salabat. Here the
merchants began to unload their goods, and the captain,
seeing that I had nothing to do, came up to me.

"I have some goods here belonging to a man that has
died," he said. "If you like to trade with them, I will pay
you for your trouble. The money I get from the goods I
shall take to the dead man's family."

I consented, for I was glad of something to do. I took
the goods to the clerk of the ship, whose duty it was to
enter in a book the number of bales, and the names of
the merchants to whom they belonged. I presented my
bales to him, and asked the captain what was the name
of the merchant who had once possessed them.

"Enter them in the name of Sindbad," said the captain.
I was astonished to hear my own name, as you may
imagine. I looked closely at the captain, and found, to
my great amazement, that he was no other than the one
in whose ship I had sailed on my second voyage, and
who had left me on the island of fruit trees, when I had
fallen asleep! He had much altered since I had last seen
him, but there was no doubt that it was he.

"Was the merchant's name really Sindbad?" I asked.

"Yes," answered the captain. "He embarked on my ship, and sailed with me for some time. Then he, with some others, landed on an island. When we set sail again, he was left behind by mistake. His loss was not discovered till some hours later, and by that time we were driving before a strong wind, and could not return."

"You believe him to be dead, then?" I asked.

"Certainly I do," he answered.

"Now, captain," I said. "I beg you to look at me closely, and you will see that I am that Sindbad whom you left behind. I fell asleep by the brook, and when I awoke the ship was gone."

The captain looked at me in astonishment, and very soon he knew me again. He embraced me with delight, and bade me take my goods, together with the profit he had made on them.

I made much money on my homeward journey, and when I again returned to Balsora, and went from thence to Bagdad, I had so much wealth that I could not count it. I gave much to the poor, and bought another great estate. Then once again I enjoyed some years of peace and happiness.

Cannibal Island and the Friendly King

Not even the charms of wealth and greatness could stop me from embarking on a fourth voyage. I had a fine journey until one day when our ship was right out at sea. A sudden gust of wind came, and we furled our sails quickly.

It was too late. The sails were torn to rags, and the ship driven on to a sandbank. Many of my comrades perished, but I and a few others got hold of a plank. We were carried to an island, and there we found fruit and spring water, which saved us from perishing.

When we walked inland, we came to some houses. Suddenly a number of men rushed out, seized us, and carried us off. We were made to sit down, and given a certain herb to eat. My five companions, not noticing that the men ate none themselves, swallowed the herb greedily. I would not even taste mine, and it was good for me that I did not – for the effect of the herb was to make a man lose his wits and talk nonsense.

After giving us the herb, the men brought forth much rice, prepared with oil of cocoa. My comrades ate all of this, poor wretches, not having sense enough to guess that these men were eaters of men; they did not see, as I did, that they were being made fat in order to be eaten. The herb had robbed them of their senses.

When they had become fat, the men ate them. But as for me, I would not touch my food, and became thinner every day.

No one took much notice of me, and I was allowed to go where I pleased; so it was not difficult for me to escape. I chose a day when all the men were away, except for one old man. Then I set out to run as fast as I could away from the cannibals.

I traveled for seven days, living mostly on coconuts, and on the eighth I came near the sea. Suddenly I saw a great many people like myself, gathering pepper, which grew plentifully in that place.

I went to meet them, and they gathered round me, marveling at my story. Then, when they had finished plucking the pepper, they set sail in their ship, taking me with them. They went to an island, and presented me to their king, who was a good and noble prince.

The island was a fine place to live in, for there was plenty of everything, and much trade was done with ships that came to the port. I was very happy there, especially as the king showed me much favor.

I noticed a very curious thing, while I was in that land, and that was that no one, not even the king himself, used bridle, saddle, or stirrups when riding a horse. I went to the king and asked him why.

"I do not know what you mean by saddle and bridle and stirrups," he said, puzzled. "What are these things? They are unknown in my country."

I immediately went to a workman, and told him exactly how to make a saddle, which I myself covered with gold-embroidered leather. Then I had some stirrups and a bridle made, all of which I presented to the king. I put them upon one of his horses, and when he mounted, he was so delighted with them that he made me handsome presents.

It was not long before I had made many saddles and bridles for all the nobles of the court, and soon I became rich and famous. Then one day the king called me to him and spoke to me.

"Sindbad, I love you," he said. "I wish you to do something for me."

"What is that?" I asked.

"I wish you to marry a lady of my land," he said. "Then you will settle down in my kingdom, and forget all about your own country."

I did not wish to do this, but I dared not disobey the king. Soon I was given a beautiful maiden for wife, and I lived with her in a lovely house. But I could never forget my own countrymen, and longed to return to my home.

One day a friend of mine sent me bad news. His wife had fallen ill and died. I hastened to comfort him.

"God preserve you." I said, when I saw him, "and may he grant you a long life!"

"What do you mean?" he asked in surprise. "Do you not know that I have only one hour more to live?"

"How is that?" I asked.

"It is the custom in this country to bury the live husband with the dead wife," he answered.

This filled me with horror, for, I thought, if my wife

should die, I should meet my own death too.

For many days I was full of fear lest this should happen. Then, alas! what I feared came to pass. My wife fell ill, and in a short time she died.

There was no help for me. The king said that although I was a stranger to the country, I must keep to the customs, for I had married one of his ladies. Therefore, when the time came for my wife to be buried, I was taken too. The cavalcade went up the mountains, and in my despair I suddenly broke away and ran for my life.

I came to a pit whose top was covered by a stone. I lifted it up, and let myself down. No one discovered me, and I stayed there for several days. Then something came blundering against me in the dark. It was some sea animal that had come up from the sea-shore, which I had not known was near.

I followed the creature along a narrow, winding passage, which pierced through the heart of

the mountain right down to the sea. How thankful I was to see daylight again, and to breathe the fresh sea air!

For two or three days I stayed on the sea-shore. Then I saw a vessel that had left the port of the island, and I hailed her. She saw me, and sent a boat to bring me to her. I told the captain I had been shipwrecked, for I did not want him to send me back to the king. Happily, he believed my story, and allowed me to sail with him on his ship.

We went to many ports, and by good fortune I did some profitable trade with goods that the captain kindly gave me. When at last I arrived at Balsora again, I had infinite riches, and was able to make great gifts to the poor and to the church. Then I settled down happily to enjoy my kindred and friends, eager to forget how near I had been to death.

The Old Man of the Sea

After some time I decided to build myself a ship, and go voyaging once more. When my vessel was ready, I embarked on board, taking with me many other merchants and their goods.

We sailed with a fair wind, and were some weeks on the open sea. The first place we came to was a desert island, and there we found an enormous egg. It was a roc egg, and the young bird inside was on the point of hatching.

"Do not meddle with the egg," I warned the merchants who were with me. "The parent rocs are dangerous."

But they took no heed of my words. They broke open the egg with their hatchets, dragged out the young bird piece by piece, and roasted it.

They had hardly finished their feasting when two large black clouds appeared in the sky.

"Here are the parent rocs!" shouted the captain. "Let us embark again with all speed before they try to revenge themselves on us!"

We hurriedly re-embarked and set sail. We watched the two rocs find their broken egg, and heard them bewail it with a terrible noise. Then suddenly they arose in the air, and flew off in the direction from which they had come. We sailed away as fast as we could, but alas! It was of no use.

Soon the giant birds returned, each one holding in its beak a tremendous stone. They flew immediately above our vessel, and one dropped its stone. If the steersman had not cleverly turned our ship about, we should have been struck. Then the other roc dropped the stone it held. It fell right on to our vessel, split it into a thousand pieces, and sank it. All the merchants on board were either killed or sunk.

I sank down through the water, but was able to take hold of a piece of wood. I swam with this to an island,

and got ashore. I found that there were trees everywhere, full of delicious fruit – indeed the island was like a beautiful garden.

As I wandered inland, I saw an old man sitting upon the bank of a stream. I thought he must have been shipwrecked like myself, and I went forward to greet him. He did not speak in reply, but signed to me to take him upon my back, pointing over the stream as if he wished to cross the water, and gather fruit on the other side.

He seemed very weak and feeble, so I placed him on my back, and carried him across the stream. Then I bade him get down, and stooped so that he might do so. But instead he slipped his legs round my neck, and gripped me so tightly with them that I was nearly strangled. I saw that his skin was like that of a cow, and then, so tightly did he clasp his legs round my throat that I fell to the ground in a faint.

When I came to my senses, the old man was still about

my neck. He kicked me roughly, and made me get up. I did so, and he forced me to walk about under the fruit trees, so that he might pick what he wanted.

I had no rest from him that day, but was forced to carry him about with me all the time. When night came, and I lay down, he lay down with me, but would not leave go his hold on my throat.

Every day I spent in the same way, carrying the horrible old creature about with me. I led a miserable life, and could not think how to get rid of him.

Then one day I found some empty gourds. I took up the largest and cleaned it. Then I pressed into it some grapes, and I left the juice there for some days. When I next came to the gourd, I drank the grape-wine I had made, and found it so good that I sang and shouted with joy.

The old man signed to me to give him some. I made

him a gourd-full, and he drank it all off at once. He was not used to the drink, and it stupefied him and made him sleepy. When I found that he did not grip me so tightly with his legs, I gave a sudden jolt, and jerked him to the ground. He lay there without moving, and taking up a stone I slew the wicked creature without pity.

I ran down to the seashore, rejoicing with all my heart that I was free of my horrible burden. On the beach I met the crew of a ship who had landed to take in water. They were amazed to see me, and to hear my adventure.

"You fell into the hands of the Old Man of the Sea," they said. "No man has ever escaped from him before. He has strangled many hundreds of poor shipwrecked sailors, and richly deserved his death."

I put to sea with the crew, and soon we came to a great city. Here one of the merchants of the ship, with whom I had become friends, gave me a great bag.

"Go with the folk of this city," he said, "and they will take you to gather coconuts. Thus you will be able to obtain goods which you can trade in other places."

I took the bag, and went with the townsfolk, who were likewise laden with bags. We set out on a journey, and after a time came to a forest of great, tall trees, whose trunks were so smooth that it was impossible to climb them to reach the fruit.

I wondered how we were to get the coconuts, but it was not long before I saw the way. The trees were full of monkeys, who seemed very angry at our arrival. The merchants took up stones, and flung them at the furious animals. This enraged them to such an extent that they plucked the coconuts and threw them down at us. Thus all we had to do was to gather up the nuts and place them in our bags. We soon had a great number, as you can imagine.

I spent many days in this way, till I had a vast amount of nuts. Then, when a ship called into the port, I embarked on board, taking my coconuts with me. We sailed to the Isles of Comari, where I exchanged my goods for pepper and wood of aloes. I then hired divers to go pearl-fishing for me, and they brought me up some very large, pure pearls.

With these goods I sailed to Balsora, and when I again reached Bagdad I sold my pepper, wood of aloes, and pearls for vast sums. I then gave away the tenth of my wealth to the poor, and once more settled down to enjoy my riches.

The Hill of the Elephants

For some time I enjoyed a quiet life. Then one day the Caliph sent for me, and I hastened to his court.

"Sindbad," he said, "I wish you to take ship and return to the King of the Isle of Serendid, taking with you a letter from me and some rich presents."

I was full of dismay when I heard this, for I had no

wish for any more voyages or adventures. But the caliph commanded that I should go, so I dared not disobey.

Once again I went to Balsora, and embarked on a ship. I had a very happy voyage, and arrived quite safely at Serendid. The king was delighted to see me again, and was much pleased to receive the caliph's letter and gifts.

The time soon came for me to depart once more. I bade farewell to the king, who gave me a rich present for myself, and then embarked to return speedily to Balsora.

But on the way much misfortunate came upon us. Pirates attacked our ship, and took it. Those that defended themselves were killed, but I and some others who remained quiet were spared. We were all stripped of our clothes and given horrible rags to wear. Then the pirates took us to a far-off land and sold us as slaves.

A rich merchant bought me, and treated me well. He asked me if I knew any trade that I could follow.

"I am a merchant," I replied. "The pirates robbed me, and took me prisoner."

"Can you shoot with bow and arrows?" he asked.

"I used to, when I was young," I answered. "I do not think I have forgotten how to do so, even now."

My master thereupon gave me a bow and arrows, put me behind him on an elephant, and took me to a great forest. At last he stopped, and showed me a large tree.

"Climb up the tree," he said. "Elephants will come by,

and you must shoot them. If you kill one, come and tell me."

He left me there, and returned the way he had come. The next morning a great number of elephants came by. I shot my arrows among them, and slew one. When the great beasts had all gone, I ran to tell my master, who was full of joy to think that I had already killed an elephant for him.

We returned to the forest, and dug a hole in which we buried the great creature, for my master meant to come and get the ivory tusks later. Then he bade me climb my tree again, and continue my shooting.

For two months I did this, and shot many elephants. Then one day a dreadful thing happened. All the elephants in the forest came to my tree, and stood around me!

The earth shook under their feet, and the noise was terrible. They surrounded my tree, and stood staring at me, with their great trunks stretched out. I was so frightened that my bow and arrows fell from my hands.

Then the biggest of the elephants advanced to my tree, and wrapped his trunk around it. He pulled it straight up by the roots, and flung it to the ground. I fell with it, and lay like a dead man. The elephant picked me up, and put me on his back, then started off through the forest, followed by all the rest.

I was too terrified to move, and thought surely I was going to my death. After some time I felt myself being put down on the ground. Then all the elephants went away and left me by myself.

I sat up and looked around me. Imagine my astonishment when I saw that I was on a long, high hill, covered with the bones and tusks of hundreds of elephants!

"This must be the hill where they come to die!" I cried. "Oh, the wise beasts! They have brought me here to show me that I can get tusks from dead animals, and so do not need to slay the living!"

I at once went to seek my master, and after traveling for twenty-four hours. I came to him. He was delighted to see me, having thought that I had been killed by the elephants, like most of his other slaves.

When I took him to the hill of the elephants, he was filled with astonishment and delight.

"Now my fortune is made!" he cried. "And yours too, O Sindbad, for I will see to that myself!"

We spent some months in filling his warehouses with ivory, and then, when a ship called at the port, I went aboard, meaning to return home. My master gave me a great cargo of ivory and many rich presents. Then I set sail, rejoicing that my adventure had ended so well.

As soon as my ship touched at the mainland I went ashore, for I thought I would prefer to go overland to Balsora, rather than over sea, for I did not know what other strange adventure might come to me on the water. I sold my ivory, and with the great sums I got by it, I bought wonderful presents for my friends.

Then I set out in company with a large caravan of merchants, and at last came safely to Bagdad. I went at once to the caliph, who was glad to see me, for he had thought I must be dead, since I was such a long time away.

And now, for the last time, I settled down in peace and happiness, resolved never again to set out on a voyage. Thus ends the last adventure of old Sindbad the Sailor.

Aladdin and the Wonderful Lamp

There once lived in China a lazy boy called Aladdin. He was the despair of his poor mother, for he would not work, but ran about the streets all day long. His father was dead, so his mother was forced to work for them both.

One day a magician came to the city. He saw Aladdin, and looked at him closely.

"This lad will do well for my purpose," he said. "I will pretend to be his uncle, then he will obey me, and do what I wish."

So he went up to Aladdin and embraced him, saying, with tears in his eyes, that he was his uncle, and had come to find the wife and son of his dear brother, whom he had heard was now dead.

Aladdin was delighted to think he had an uncle who was richly dressed, and who might be wealthy and generous. He took him home to his mother, and the magician paid for a splendid meal.

"I will set Aladdin up in a fine shop," he promised. "I will come tomorrow and take him to a tailor's, where I will buy him a magnificent new suit."

Aladdin and his mother were so overjoyed that they could hardly sleep that night. In the morning the magician came as he had promised, and bought Aladdin a richly embroidered robe.

"Now we will go walking," he said. "I want to give you some advice, nephew, and therefore we will spend the day together."

He took Aladdin through the city, talking to him wisely all the time, as an uncle might talk to his favorite nephew. At last they passed right out of the city and came to the country. Still the magician led Aladdin on, and only stopped when they arrived in a valley between two mountains.

"Now I am going to show you something strange that no one has seen before," said the magician. "Gather me some sticks, Aladdin, and we will light a fire."

Aladdin obeyed. Soon a great fire was blazing. The magician threw some powder upon the flames, turned himself about, and pronounced some magic words.

Suddenly the earth shook, and opened just in front of Aladdin. In the space that appeared was a stone with a brass ring in the middle. The lad was so frightened that he turned to run away, but the magician caught hold of him.

"I have brought you here to fulfill my commands." he said. "Do as you are told, and I will make you rich."

Aladdin listened in surprise. When he heard that he might be made rich, he begged his supposed uncle to tell him what he must do.

"Pull up this stone," said the magician. "Go down the
steps to the door at the end. Open it, and you will find
yourself in a beautiful palace. Go through three vast
halls, into the fourth. In a corner you will see a lamp
hanging. Take it down, and bring it to me."

Aladdin promised to do as he was bid. The magician

pulled a ring off his finger, and slipped it on Aladdin's.

"Wear this," he said. "It will keep you from harm."

The youth pulled up the stone, and saw a flight of
steps going downwards. He ran down them, and came to
a door, which he opened. He passed through it into a
beautiful palace. Through three vast halls he went, and

came to the fourth, where in a corner hung the lamp of which the magician had told him.

He took it, and fastened it to his belt. Then he saw a wonderful garden outside the hall, with trees bearing strange fruit, for they were hung with rubies, emeralds, diamonds, and sapphires. Aladdin ran to them, and filled his pockets full of the precious stones.

Then he went back to the opening where he had left the magician. The old man was awaiting him impatiently, and as soon as he saw Aladdin, he sharply commanded him to pass him the lamp.

"It is fastened to my belt," replied the lad. "Wait till I get out of here, uncle."

Then the magician flew into a rage, and ordered Aladdin to do as he was bid. But the youth would not give him the lamp until he was outside.

The magician stamped his foot in fury. He turned to the fire, which was still burning, and flung a pinch of powder on it, pronouncing two fearful words of magic at the same time. Immediately the stone closed up the entrance to the underground cave, and poor Aladdin was a prisoner!

He called and pleaded, but it was of no use. The magician had gone. Aladdin ran down the steps to enter the palace again, but found that the door to it was shut. He was indeed a prisoner. In despair he clasped his hands together, and in doing so rubbed the ring which the magician had given him.

Then a most surprising thing happened! An enormous genie rose out of the earth, and bowed down before Aladdin!

"What do you wish?" he asked. "I am the slave of the ring, and must obey you in everything."

"Then take me from this place," said Aladdin, after he had overcome his astonishment. At once the genie caught hold of him, and in a trice Aladdin found himself outside the cave, seated on the place where the stone had once been.

He made his way back to the city, and soon arrived home, where he told his mother all that had happened. Then, being very tired, he went to bed.

Next morning he awoke feeling hungry, and begged his mother to get him breakfast. She replied that there was none in the house, but she would go and sell some cotton she had made.

"Wait a moment, Mother," said Aladdin. "I have here an old lamp that I got for that wicked magician. Take it and sell it. That should bring us enough for breakfast."

"It is very dirty," said his mother. "I will polish it."

She took a rag and rubbed it hard. Immediately a gigantic genie appeared, and spoke to her in a voice of thunder.

"What do you wish? I am the slave of the lamp, and must obey you in everything."

Aladdin's mother was so frightened that she fell in a faint on the floor. Aladdin snatched the lamp from her, and gave his command to the genie.

"I am hungry," he said. "Bring me breakfast."

The genie disappeared, but soon returned again with a

large silver basin on his head, and twelve covered silver dishes containing all kinds of delicious food. These he placed before Aladdin, then bowed and disappeared.

The youth soon brought his mother to her senses, and they sat down together to enjoy the meal, marveling at the strange happenings of the last two days.

Such was the beginning of Aladdin's good fortune. He and his mother now had no lack of good things, and lived in great comfort.

Then one day Aladdin saw the sultan's daughter, the beautiful Badroulbadour. She was so charming, so lovely, so enchanting that the youth fell head over heels in love with her. Nothing would content him but that he must make her his wife.

His mother laughed when she heard this, but Aladdin would not alter his purpose. He bade her go to the sultan, taking with her the jewels he had picked from the strange trees in the underground cave. She was to give the Sultan these, and ask that the princess might become the wife of her son.

The poor woman, who felt certain that the sultan would be angry with her for asking such a thing, at last agreed to go. She put the jewels in a china dish, covered them with a damask cloth, and set off.

The sultan received her, and she uncovered the dish, begging him to accept the present that her son had sent him.

"He beseeches you to give him your daughter in marriage," she said.

The sultan hardly heard her. He was gazing at the marvelous jewels in the china dish. Never before had he seen such treasures. Each one of them was worth more than all the gold in his coffers.

"My son requests the honor of your daughter's hand in marriage," repeated Aladdin's mother, seeing the sultan's amazement.

"Tell him he shall have her if he can send me forty golden dishes full of jewels like these, carried by eighty slaves!" said the sultan.

The woman left the palace in delight, for she knew that the genie could obtain these things. She told Aladdin what the sultan had said, and he was overjoyed.

He rubbed the lamp, and when the genie appeared, he commanded him to fulfill the sultan's wish, and also to dress himself and his mother in rich and magnificent clothing. This was all done in the twinkling of an eye.

Soon the astonished people of the city saw a great procession of eighty slaves walking to the sultan's palace, and at the head were Aladdin and his mother dressed in superb robes. The sultan received them with delight, for he thought surely Aladdin must be a very great prince.

"You shall marry my daughter tomorrow," he promised. "Meanwhile, let me entertain you today in my palace."

Aladdin spent the day with the sultan. When he returned home he rubbed the wonderful lamp again, and commanded the genie to build him a marvelous palace opposite the sultan's. It was to be of silver and gold, and the windows were to be studded with precious stones. There were to be servants of all kinds, and also a treasury filled with bags of gold and silver.

In the morning the sultan was amazed to see a magnificent palace glittering in the distance. He felt more certain than ever that Aladdin must be a rich and mighty prince, and he was overjoyed to think that his daughter would have such a powerful husband.

The beautiful Princess Badroulbadour was married to Aladdin that day, and proudly he took her home with him to his palace. They were both very happy, the princess because her husband was so rich and handsome, and Aladdin because he had for a wife the sweetest and loveliest maiden in the land.

They lived happily together for some time. Then one day Aladdin went out hunting, and the princess was left alone. It so happened that the magician came into the city that morning, anxious to find out what had happened to Aladdin. He felt certain that the youth had perished in the underground cave, but he wished to make sure.

Very soon, by means of his magic art, he discovered that Aladdin had escaped, taking the wonderful lamp with him. When he came to the palace that the genie had built, he at once knew that it was a magic one, and guessed that Aladdin was the owner. He was amazed when he heard that the poor peasant boy he had left in the cave had become the sultan's son-in-law, and had won the beautiful princess for wife.

He was angry, and determined to punish Aladdin. He bought a dozen new brass lamps, and put them into a basket. Then he went slowly down the street by the palace, crying out, "new lamps for old! New lamps for old!"

At once children ran round him laughing, for they had never heard of any one giving new things for old before. Soon there was a mob around the old man, and the princess, leaning from her window, saw the crowd, and wondered what the excitement was.

Her servants told her.

"It is a peddler who is giving new lamps for old!" they said. "Mistress, there is an old lamp in your lord's room. Shall we not exchange it for a new one? Whoever owns the old will be pleased to find a new one in its place."

"Fetch it, and change it then," said the princess, anxious to see if the peddler really meant what he said.

No sooner did the magician see the servant bringing out the old lamp to him than he knew it was the one he wanted. He seized it, threw a new one at the girl, and hurried away.

When he came to a quiet corner he rubbed it. At once the genie appeared, and was commanded to transport Aladdin's palace into the middle of the desert. This he did, much to the fear and astonishment of the princess and her ladies.

The sultan was amazed to see the palace gone. When Aladdin returned from the hunt, he too was filled with astonishment. He soon guessed what had happened, and resolved to defeat the magician as soon as possible.

He rubbed the ring on his finger, and when the slave appeared he commanded him to bring the palace back again.

"Lord, I am not so mighty as the slave of the lamp," answered the genie. "I cannot do that."

"Then take me to the place where the palace stands," said Aladdin impatiently.

This was soon done. Aladdin found himself on the steps of his own palace, and swiftly he ran up them, and made his way to the princess, who was overjoyed to see him.

"Hide behind this curtain," she said. "When the magician comes to see me, you can surprise him, and slay him."

Aladdin did as she bade him. When he heard the magician enter, he sprang out, and without mercy slew the wicked man instantly. Then he took the wonderful lamp from him, and rubbed it.

At once the genie appeared, and bowed low.

"Take this palace back to its rightful place," commanded Aladdin. Immediately it arose in the air, and in a trice returned to its place in the city of the sultan.

How overjoyed he was to see Aladdin and the princess once again! Bells rang out through the city, and a great festival was proclaimed. All the people had a holiday and rejoiced.

When the sultan died Aladdin became ruler, and he and his lovely princess lived happily together to the end of their days.

The Enchanted Horse

Long ago, when the Emperor of Persia was holding a festival, an Indian came to the foot of the throne, and bowed himself to the ground. With him he brought a magnificent horse, which, although it looked as if it were real, was artificial.

"Lord," said the Indian, "I bring you the most wonderful thing in the world – a horse that will transport its rider through the air to any place that he wishes to go."

"Let me see this wonder," commanded the emperor. "Do you see that hill yonder? Bid your horse take you there, and, so that I shall know you have truly been there, bring me back a palm-leaf from the tree that grows at the bottom of the hill."

The Indian leapt on to the horse's back, and turned a peg in its neck. At once the wonderful thing rose up into the air, and flew like the wind to the distant hill. In a short time the Indian returned, bearing in his hand a palm-leaf.

The Emperor was amazed.

"What do you want for this wonder of yours?" he asked.

"But one thing," said the Indian. "Grant me your daughter as wife, and you shall have the horse."

The emperor's son, who was near by, was angry to hear the request of the Indian.

"What!" he cried. "Does this insolent juggler think that the princess would be given to him as wife?"

"Peace, my son," commanded the emperor. "I certainly shall not grant him his ridiculous request, but maybe I can give him something else which will please him as much. Before I make my proposal to him, mount the horse yourself, and see what you think of its powers."

The prince ran to the horse, and before the Indian could help him up, or give him any advice, he leapt into the saddle, and turned the peg in the horse's neck. At once it rose into the air, and flew away to the west.

The Indian cried out in fear, for he knew that the prince had no idea how to manage the horse. He flung himself down before the emperor, and begged him not to punish him if the prince did not return.

The emperor turned pale. He waited for the horse to bring back the prince, but it had vanished completely, and there was no sign of its return.

"Throw this Indian into prison," he commanded. "There he shall remain, and if my son does not come back, his head shall be cut off!"

The wretched Indian was flung into prison and there he lay, bewailing his fate and fearing death at any moment.

The prince at first enjoyed his ride very much. When

he thought he had been away long enough, he turned the
peg in the horse's neck again. To his surprise and fear,
the horse did not return, but went on flying higher than
ever in the sky. Soon the prince lost sight of the earth,
and could not tell where he was.

At last night came, and stars twinkled down. The
prince suddenly found another little peg, just behind the
animal's right ear. He turned it, and was delighted to

find that the horse at once began to descend.

Soon it came to rest on something hard. The prince leapt off its back, and found that he was on the flat roof of a magnificent palace wherein dwelt the Princess of Bengal. He found a flight of steps leading downwards, and descended them.

He came to a big room where many slaves lay sleeping on the floor. He tiptoed between them, and came to another room. On a raised bed lay a fair princess, more beautiful than any maiden the prince had ever seen.

He made his way softly to her bedside, and gazed on her. Then he gently touched her snow-white arm. She awoke and looked in surprise at the handsome prince by her side.

"Madam," said the prince, "do not be afraid. By the strangest adventure imaginable, I, the son of the Emperor of Persia, have arrived here at your palace. I pray you to give me your protection."

The princess listened in astonishment. Then she awoke her slaves, and bade them give the prince food and drink, and then conduct him to a bed.

"You shall tell me your story in the morning," she said.

When day dawned the princess arose and made herself even more beautiful than she was already. Then she sent for the prince to come to her, and listened in surprise to the strange tale he told her.

"You must spend some time in my kingdom before

you return," she said. This the prince was only too glad to do, for he had immediately fallen in love with the fair princess.

For two months he remained with her, and then he said that he must return to his father.

"Come with me, I beg of you," he entreated. "I love you, and would marry you. Let me take you to my father, the Emperor of Persia."

The maiden, who had fallen madly in love with the handsome prince, soon consented. Next morning, very early, they arose and went to the enchanted horse. The

prince mounted on its back, and placed the princess safely before him. Then, turning the peg in its neck, they set out on their journey through the air.

When they arrived at the kingdom of the Persian emperor, the prince made the horse descend.

"This palace at which we are now arrived is the summer palace of my father," he said. "Remain here, I pray you, until I have prepared the emperor for your coming. I will then send to fetch you."

The prince gave the enchanted horse to a groom, and then mounted one of his own horses. He rode off, and soon came to his father's city. The people gave him a great welcome, cheering him, and running beside his horse in delight.

The emperor was overjoyed to see his son again, and embraced him tenderly. When he heard of his strange adventure, he was amazed.

"We will go to fetch your princess with great pomp and splendor," he said. "Let us make ready now. In the meantime, the Indian to whom the horse belonged shall be freed."

Now, as soon as the Indian was freed, he asked what had happened. His jailer told him, and an evil plan came into the Indian's mind. He would revenge himself on the emperor and the prince!

Without delay, he ran to the summer palace, where the princess awaited the prince.

"Tell the princess that I have been sent to carry her on the enchanted horse to the prince, her lover," he said to the man guarding the animal.

The princess believed the message to be true, and at once came out and mounted the horse with the Indian. He turned the peg in the neck, and they rose into the air. As they flew off, they were seen by the emperor and the prince, who were on their way to fetch the princess.

In amazement and despair the poor prince stood and watched the Indian flying off with his lady. Then he began to weep bitterly, for he did not know where she was being taken to, nor how he should find her again.

He dressed himself as a peasant, and went wandering through many lands, seeking for his princess, but not for a long while did he obtain news of her.

Meanwhile the Indian had flown far away with the frightened maiden, who knew, as soon as she saw the prince down below, that the Indian had played her false.

After some hours, the wicked man brought the horse down into a wood, near the capital city of Cashmire.

"I will get you some food, fair lady," he said, "and then I will find someone to marry us."

"I will never marry you!" cried the princess in horror. She tried to run away but the Indian ran after her and caught her. She began to shriek for help, and happily her cries were at once heard.

The Sultan of Cashmire and his men were passing

through the wood, returning from a hunt. They ran to the fair lady's rescue, and one of the men slew the wicked Indian. The princess was full of gratitude, and thanked the sultan with all her heart.

"Come with me to my palace," said the sultan. "You shall stay there and be well looked after. Tell me your story as we ride through the wood."

The princess told her story, and the sultan looked with great interest at the enchanted horse, which he commanded to be taken along with them. As soon as they reached his palace he took the princess to some beautiful rooms, gave her a great number of slaves, and left her.

The princess felt sure that the sultan would send her back to her prince without delay, and went to bed very happily. She was awakened next morning by the sound of drums and trumpets, and asked her slaves what the joyful sounds were for.

"It is your wedding day!" they said. "The sultan, our master, means to marry you today!"

The poor princess fell back in a faint at this news. She had no idea that the sultan had fallen in love with her, and had resolved to marry her immediately. When she came to her senses she determined to pretend she was mad, and then perhaps the sultan would put off the wedding.

So she said strange things, and flew at every one who came near her. He slaves were dismayed, and sent word to the sultan. The princess sang and gabbled and made as if she would fly at him too, so that he departed in horror, and gave orders that the marriage was not to be held until the princess was better.

But she became worse rather than better, and the sultan sent for the wisest doctors in the land. They could do nothing with her, and gave her up in despair, for they did not guess that her madness was all a pretence.

One day the prince, who was still seeking for his lady, heard news of a princess of Bengal who was mad, and wondered if it could be his long-lost love. He made his way to Cashmire, and at last came to the sultan's city. He sent word to him that he thought he could cure the princess if he could have a little time alone with her.

The sultan, eager to try anyone's skill, consented to this. The prince, disguised as a doctor, entered the room where the princess sat. She made as if she would fly at him, but he spoke softly to her.

"I am your own prince," he said. "I come to rescue you. Do not show that you know me, in case anyone is spying upon us."

The princess was overjoyed. She sat quietly, and the prince, in a low voice, told her all his tale. Then he went to speak with the sultan.

"Lord," he said, "how comes it that the Princess of Bengal should be here, so far from her own country?"

"She came on an enchanted horse," answered the

sultan. "I have it here still."

"Ah!" said the prince, who had made a cunning plan. "Now I see what is the cause of the princess's illness. Some of the horse's enchantment has entered into her and made her mad. I can cure her, if you will permit me to mount her upon the horse, while I use my magic nearby."

The sultan promised to do all that the prince wished, for he was full of happiness to think that the princess might soon be well enough to marry him.

"Bring out the enchanted horse and stand it in the great square of the city," said the prince. "Then bid the princess dress herself richly, and adorn herself with the most beautiful jewels that you possess. Proclaim to your people that the princess is to be cured, and let them come to see the sight, for it will be a marvelous one."

All was done as the prince commanded. The horse was brought out into the great square, and every one assembled to see the princess cured. Soon she herself appeared, covered with jewels. The prince took her hand, and led her to the horse. She mounted it, and sat there, waiting.

Then the prince caused a great many vessels full of fire to be placed round the horse. He threw on the flames a powder which sent out a strong smell and a dark smoke. Then he ran round the horse three times, pretending to mutter magic words.

By this time the vessels had sent out such dense
clouds of smoke that neither the horse nor the princess
could be seen. The prince jumped up behind his lady,
turned the peg in the horse's neck, and it at once rose
into the air!

The sultan saw them when they were high up, and
was filled with the most terrible rage and grief. But he
could do nothing.

It was not long before the prince and princess arrived
in Persia, and were greatly welcomed by the emperor
and all his people. They were married that same day, and
every one rejoiced at their happiness. They dwelt
together in great content, and were happy to the end of
their days.

Ali Baba and the Forty Thieves

There once lived two brothers called Cassim and Ali Baba. One was rich and the other was poor. Ali was the poor brother, and got his living by cutting wood in the forest nearby, and carrying it into the town upon his three asses.

One day, when he had loaded his asses, he saw a crowd of well-armed, well-mounted horsemen coming in the distance. He at once guessed them to be robbers, and in a panic he hid his asses, and climbed up a tree that grew above a large rock in the hillside.

There he hid, hoping that the robbers would pass by without seeing him. To his surprise they rode right up to the rock over which his tree grew, and dismounted. The leader went up to the rock and said, in a loud and commanding voice: "Open Sesame!"

At once the rock slid aside, showing an opening. The robbers disappeared inside, and did not come out for some time. When they did, they galloped away.

Ali Baba slid down from the tree, and ran to the rock. "Open Sesame!" he cried. The rock slid aside again, and lo and behold! Instead of a gloomy cavern, Ali Baba saw a spacious room in which were piled gold, silver, jewels, brocades, and silks.

Ali hurriedly took as many bags of gold as his three asses would carry, and went to the entrance of the cave. He found that it was shut, but when he pronounced the words "Open Sesame!" again, the rock once more opened, and he ran out. It closed behind him, and Ali Baba looked for his three asses. He loaded them with the bags of gold, and then set off for the town.

When he undid the bags and showed his wife all the gold he had brought, she was so astonished that she could not speak a word.

"Let us bury it in the garden tonight," she said at last. "But first I must know how much we have. There is too much to count, so I will borrow a measure from your brother Cassim's wife, and measure it."

She ran to borrow what she wanted. Cassim's wife, knowing how poor Ali Baba was, wondered what he needed a measure for. So, being a curious woman, she put a little suet at the bottom of her measure, hoping that a little of whatever Ali was measuring would stick to the bottom, and so tell her what she wanted to know.

Ali's wife measured the gold, and then went to return the measure. Judge of the astonishment of Cassim's wife when she found a gold piece sticking to the bottom of her measure! She at once ran to Cassim and showed him.

"Your brother must be far richer than you are if he has to measure his gold, instead of counting it," she said. "Go and find out where he gets it from."

So Cassim went to Ali Baba, and told him what his wife had found.

"I am your brother," he said. "You must share your good fortune with me."

Then Ali Baba, who was always good-tempered, and willing to do any one a good turn, told his brother everything, even to the words that opened the treasure cave.

Cassim at once resolved to go to the cave before Ali Baba went again, and take from it all the treasure there was. So next morning, very early, he saddled his ass, and rode off, followed by ten mules, each carrying a large empty chest. He easily found the rock, and on saying the words "Open Sesame!" saw it open, and display the treasure cave.

He went in, overjoyed to see so much wealth. The door shut behind him, but as he knew the word to open it again he thought nothing of it. He began to get together all the gold and jewels he could see. When he had got enough to fill the ten chests, he went to the rock that closed the entrance of the cave.

Then alas for Cassim! He could not remember the words that opened the cave! Sesame was the name of a certain grain, and Cassim, remembering that he must say the name of a grain, said "Open Barley!"

The rock remained shut. Then Cassim tried again.

"Open Oats!" he shouted. But the rock did not move.

Cassim fell into a panic, and shouted the names of all the grains he could think of, but never once did he hit on the right one.

After some time, the robbers returned, and saw the ten mules outside the cave. They at once knew that someone was inside. The captain, as soon as the rock opened at his command, rushed and slew poor Cassim.

"Maybe he is the only one who knows our secret," he said. "But in case anyone else shares it with him, we will show how dreadful our revenge is. We will cut this man's body into four pieces, and put two on each side of the door to warn any intruder of our severity."

This was done, and the robbers once more rode off.

Now Cassim's wife began to get very uneasy when her husband did not come back. She sent for Ali Baba and begged him to go to the cave, and see if he was there. Ali went at once, and when he found the body of his brother, he was full of sorrow.

"We must let no one know of this," he said to Cassim's weeping wife. 'You must say that he died of an illness. Tomorrow we will give him a funeral, but first I must find someone who will sew the four pieces together, so that my poor brother may rest in peace."

Ali Baba did not dare to go out and find someone himself, so he let Morgiana, a slave of Cassim's, into the dreadful secret. The girl promised to do all she could, and ran out to find a cobbler. Soon she came to one called Baba Mustapha, who sat in the market mending shoes.

"Come with me," she said, "I have a piece of work for you. See, here is a gold coin. You will have another when the work is finished. But I must bind your eyes, Baba Mustapha, for you must not know to what place you are going."

The old cobbler consented. Morgiana bound his eyes, and led him to her dead master's house. There she bade him sew the four pieces together, which he did neatly and quickly. Then she bound his eyes, and led him back to his stall again.

Cassim was given a fine funeral, and no one guessed that he had been killed by robbers; all thought he had died of an illness. Ali Baba moved to Cassim's house, and he and his wife enjoyed their new riches.

Now when the robbers discovered that Cassim's body had been taken away, they were in a fright, for they knew that someone had learned of their hiding-place, and was taking away their gold.

"One of you must dress as a traveler, and go into the town to see if you can hear of anyone who has been cut to pieces," said the captain. "Then we shall soon find his friend or his brother, or whoever it is that has taken away the body."

So one of the robbers disguised himself, and set off in

the early morning. It happened that he stood by Baba Mustapha's stall, when he entered the market, and he watched the old man's nimble fingers with admiration.

"Old man," he said, "you must have good eyes to see so well at your stitching, for indeed it is hardly light yet."

The cobbler laughed. "My eyes are as good as my fingers!" he boasted. "Why, my friend, I sewed together a body the other day, and had not as much light to do so as there is now!"

The robber looked at him sharply, for he knew that by chance he had hit on the right person to help him.

"Tell me more about this," he said.

But Baba Mustapha would say nothing further.

"Lead me to this place, and I will give you gold," said the robber.

"I was blindfolded, so I do not know where it was," said Mustapha.

"Here is gold," said the robber. "Let me blindfold you, and maybe you can remember the way."

He at last won the cobbler's consent, and the old man led the way blindfolded to Cassim's house, where Ali Baba now lived. The robber marked the door with a white cross, and rewarded his guide with more gold. Then he ran to tell the captain of his discovery.

Now Morgiana, the slave, happening to come out of the house on an errand, noticed the white cross on the door. "This bodes no good for my master," she thought.

So, taking a piece of white chalk, she made crosses on many other doors up and down the street.

When the robber captain came to find the door he was astonished to find a great many with white crosses on,

and could not, of course, discover in which house lived the man who knew his secret. In rage he returned to his men and slew the wretched robber who had marked the door with a cross. Then he sent a second man to the cobbler.

Baba Mustapha, blindfolded, led him to the door of Ali's house. He marked it with a tiny red cross in the corner, and returned rejoicing to his master. But Morgiana, who was now on the look-out, saw the cross with her sharp eyes, and immediately marked all the other doors nearby in the same way.

The robber captain was full of rage when he saw this, and he slew the second robber. Then he determined to go to the town himself and find out. So once again the old cobbler led a robber to Ali Baba's door. This time there was no cross made, for the captain simply examined it very carefully, till he felt certain he would know it again; then he returned to his men.

"Go and buy nineteen mules and thirty-eight oil-jars," he commanded. "Fill one with oil, and then come to me."

This was done. The captain made his thirty-seven men get into the oil-jars, and then he tied up the tops of them. He loaded the nineteen mules with two jars each and set off to go to Ali Baba's, meaning to ask for a night's shelter there, and then slay all who were in the house.

Ali Baba willingly gave the supposed oil merchant shelter, and told him to put his jars in the yard. The captain commanded his men to leap out as soon as he called them, and then left them.

Now Morgiana the slave was preparing a fine dinner for her master and his guest. As she was in the middle of it, her lamp went out, for there was no more oil left. She remembered that there were oil jars in the yard, and picking up her lamp, she ran out to fill it from a jar.

As she ran to one, a voice spoke from within it. "Is it time?" said the voice.

Then Morgiana guessed that the oil merchant was not

what he seemed, and as soon as she had heard voices from thirty-seven of the jars, each asking the same question, she knew that her master's guest was the captain of the thieves, who had brought his robbers with him. To every man she answered. "Not yet, but presently," then she filled her lamp from the one real jar of oil and ran to the kitchen.

She took her big kettle and filled it with oil, which she boiled over the fire. Then, running to every jar containing a robber, she poured in enough oil to stifle and kill him. This done, she went on with her preparation of the dinner.

The captain thought that the time had now come to call his men. He went to the room that had been given to him, and leaned from the window.

"It is time," he called, in a low voice. There was no answer. He called again – and then, surprised and dismayed, ran into the yard. He peeped into the jars and found all his men dead. Then, full of fear, he went back to the house again, determined to kill Ali Baba as soon as the meal was finished.

Morgiana served the dinner, and saw that the supposed oil merchant had a dagger in his clothing. She retired, and dressed herself as a dancer. Then, taking a tambourine in her hand, she went before her master and his guest, and bowed.

She began to dance, which she could do very well. As she circled round the room, she drew a dagger, and flourished it here and there, as if it were part of the dance. Then, when she had finished, she ran to Ali Baba and held out her tambourine to him.

He put in a piece of gold. She turned to the oil merchant, and held it out to him, holding her dagger in the other hand – then, before he knew what was happening, she struck him to the heart, and the wicked man fell dead before her.

"What do you mean by this!" cried Ali Baba in a rage. But Morgiana, stripped off the captain's beard and outer garments, showed him – the captain of the robbers.

"Now you are indeed a clever maiden!" cried Ali Baba. "You shall marry my nephew, and I will set you up for life!"

"Come and see the jars that the merchant brought with him," said Morgiana. Ali Baba praised the clever slave with all his heart when he saw how she had saved him and his family from destruction, and at once caused her to be married to his nephew, who, on his part, was delighted to have such a pretty and clever maiden for his bride.

Ali Baba and his sons lived in wealth and happiness all their lives, using the treasure cave whenever they needed more riches, for now that the robbers had been killed, there was nothing more to fear.